S0-BQX-180

DEC 2015

Search and Rescue Animals

Precious McKenzie

rourkeeducationalmedia.com

Before Reading:

Building Academic Vocabulary and Background Knowledge

Before reading a book, it is important to tap into what your child or students already know about the topic. This will help them develop their vocabulary, increase their reading comprehension, and make connections across the curriculum.

1. *Look at the cover of the book. What will this book be about?*
2. *What do you already know about the topic?*
3. *Let's study the Table of Contents. What will you learn about in the book's chapters?*
4. *What would you like to learn about this topic? Do you think you might learn about it from this book? Why or why not?*
5. *Use a reading journal to write about your knowledge of this topic. Record what you already know about the topic and what you hope to learn about the topic.*
6. *Read the book.*
7. *In your reading journal, record what you learned about the topic and your response to the book.*
8. *After reading the book complete the activities below.*

Content Area Vocabulary
Read the list. What do these words mean?

assist
avalanche
canines
drowning
equine
first responders
impulses
laboratory
scent
skin cells
training
volunteers

After Reading:

Comprehension and Extension Activity

After reading the book, work on the following questions with your child or students in order to check their level of reading comprehension and content mastery.

1. *What types of situations call for SAR animals? (Summarize)*
2. *What skills are needed in a SAR team? (Asking questions)*
3. *Do you have the skills and interests to be part of a SAR team? Explain. (Text to self connection)*
4. *Explain the difference between a tracking dog and a trailing dog? (Summarize)*
5. *Why do people volunteer to be a part of a SAR team? (Asking questions)*

Extension Activity
Be prepared! SAR teams are dispatched during an emergency or natural disaster such as tornados, hurricanes, or blizzards. Think about the natural disasters that could happen in your area. Are you prepared? Do you have a plan in place at school or at home? You will create a disaster plan poster to share with your family or classmates. Use www.fema.gov to help you identify what you need to do before, during, and after a natural disaster strikes.

Table of Contents

Chapter 1
Emergency!

Help! Help! What should you do in an emergency? Call 9-1-1!

Did you know that in some emergencies highly trained teams, made up of people and animals, are the **first responders** to a 9-1-1 call?

If people are reported lost or hurt, search and rescue teams are ready to **assist**.

Search and Rescue teams consist of an animal and a handler. Both the animal and handler must be dedicated in their work and training to help others.

With their intense **training**, search and rescue teams perform amazing rescues under the most difficult situations. Their hard work and bravery save thousands of lives every year.

Approximately 300 dogs were used in the aftermath of the September 11, 2001 attacks. These dogs were well trained in agility and focus. They were not afraid to enter into the collapsed buildings to search for survivors.

Although most search and rescue dogs think of their jobs as play, it's not easy. Training begins when dogs are still puppies. Most of the dogs are not ready for their first mission until they've trained for at least two years.

Chapter 2
SAR Dogs

Search and rescue dogs, or SAR dogs, specialize in trailing, tracking, or air-scenting. Air-scenting dogs look for any sign of human **scent** in the air. They can close in on the scent even when the missing person's track is long gone.

Trailing dogs, however, look for the path of a lost person by following tiny particles of the human's **skin cells**. Trailing dogs must follow one person's scent and find that person. The dogs can use air or ground clues to help them.

Bloodhounds can scent discriminate. That means Bloodhounds can find one specific person based on the person's unique scent.

Tracking dogs actually track a person's path. Imagine footprints in the mud. A tracking dog will see the footprints, stick his nose to the ground, and use both his eyes and his nose to follow the person's footprints until he either finds the person or loses the path.

Team Member: Firefighter Matt
Dog: Buster

Search and rescue teams are trained in CPR and first aid. Many are also firefighters, paramedics, or police officers.

Chapter 3
Disaster Dogs

When a tornado or other natural disaster strikes, search and rescue teams locate missing people. Quick moving **canines** waste no time. They know they must find the victims before it is too late.

A dog's sense of smell is 50 times better than a human's. That's why dogs can pick up and track scents for long distances.

One of the most dangerous places you'll find a SAR dog is on a snowy mountain, after an **avalanche**. Their keen sense of smell and excellent hearing help rescuers find people buried under the snow. Plus, SAR dogs move faster than humans in the snow. A SAR dog can search a two and a half acre (one hectare) area in thirty minutes. It would take twenty people almost four hours to do the same job.

When a trained avalanche rescue dog finds the missing person, the dog starts digging and barking. The rescue team must uncover the person as quickly as possible before the person runs out of air to breathe.

Was there an accident in the water? Call in the search and rescue team! SAR dogs hop into a boat or track near the water's edge to find **drowning** victims. The dogs use their keen sense of smell to pinpoint where a human body is located under the water.

A SAR water dog must be able to ride in a boat and not fall overboard. The handler needs to be aware of the water's depth, tide, and current in order to keep the team safe while searching the water.

Cadaver dogs don't just solve crimes. Cadaver dogs have been used to help historians locate old burial grounds and learn more about the history of an area.

SAR cadaver dogs work with police officers to collect evidence and solve cases. These dogs use their noses to help police officers locate bodies and bones. SAR cadaver dogs can find bodies buried 15 feet (4.5 meters) underground, with a 95 percent accuracy rate.

When called to duty, SAR dogs and their handlers don't waste a minute. They load their gear and head to the scene. The teams will work 12 hour-days, with little time for rest. Many teams are made up of **volunteers**. They receive no pay for their work. They do it because they know their skills might save a life.

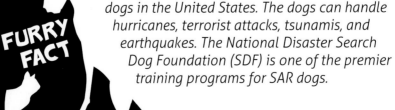

FURRY FACT

FEMA has certified 263 search and rescue (SAR) dogs in the United States. The dogs can handle hurricanes, terrorist attacks, tsunamis, and earthquakes. The National Disaster Search Dog Foundation (SDF) is one of the premier training programs for SAR dogs.

Do You Have What It Takes to Be a SAR Handler?
Check and see if you can do the following:

 **Read Maps**

 **Use a Compass**

 Use Radios to Communicate

 **Perform CPR**

 **Give First Aid**

 **Enjoy Working Outdoors**

Chapter 4
Non-canine SAR Critters

When emergencies happen over rugged terrain or deep in the wilderness, **equine** SAR teams are called in to help. With their strong senses of hearing, sight, and smell, horses make excellent SAR animals. Their height also helps searchers see across fields and over long distances.

SAR horses carry supplies, gear, and first aid equipment for search and rescue workers. And, SAR horses can carry people for many miles, allowing rescuers to work longer and travel farther than if they were traveling on their own two feet.

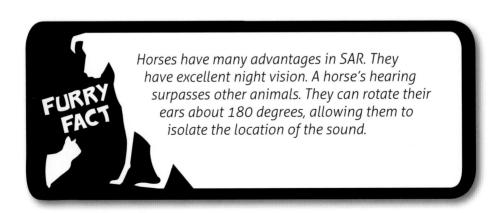

FURRY FACT

Horses have many advantages in SAR. They have excellent night vision. A horse's hearing surpasses other animals. They can rotate their ears about 180 degrees, allowing them to isolate the location of the sound.

People who volunteer for SAR mounted rescues usually train and use their own horses. Many are certified in mounted search and rescue by the National Association for Search and Rescue (NASAR).

17

Finding the right animals to work on search and rescue missions is not an easy task. It can be a very long process. For example, in the 1940s, a Tufts University **laboratory** found that pigeons could easily recognize shapes and colors. Then,

MAKE SURE YOU HAVE SOMETHING ORANGE, RED OR YELLOW WITH YOU WHEN YOU'RE BOATING, SO I CAN FIND YOU, WHEN YOU NEED HELP.

U.S. COAST GUARD SEARCH AND RESCUE

because of this research, in the 1970s and 1980s, the United States Coast Guard thought pigeons might be helpful in search and rescue missions. After training pigeons and taking them on test missions, the Coast Guard found that the pigeons could spot objects in the water with a 93 percent accuracy rate, far better than the human crews! Sadly, the Coast Guard had two helicopter crashes that destroyed the pigeon system. Due to cuts in government spending, the pigeon SAR work was stopped completely in 1983.

When the pigeons would spot an object in the water, the pigeons would peck a key that would then send a message to the helicopter pilot, alerting him that there was an object in the water below.

Now scientists are studying ways to use rats and cockroaches in search and rescue efforts. With the use of computer technology, scientists have experimented with "computer backpacks" for Madagascar Hissing Cockroaches. The scientists use a joystick to send radio signals to the backpack that is attached to the cockroach. The backpack gives out electrical **impulses** to the cockroach and the cockroach moves left or right, depending on where the signal came from. The scientists want to use these cockroaches for getting into those deep, dark places, under rubble, in search and rescue missions.

FURRY FACT

The U.S. Army is researching ways to use rats as land mine detectors, explosive detectors, and possibly as search and rescue workers. Their small size and light weight might make them ideal for this type of work.

Chapter 5

Support Search and Rescue

Search and rescue animals are always there to help in an emergency. The animals use their sharp senses to find missing persons and rescue those in danger. Each year, many people owe their lives to the brave work SAR teams perform. When you meet a SAR hero team, be sure to thank them for their courage and hard work.

Former Secretary of the Department of Homeland Security, Janet Napolitano, made SAR teams an important part of her job success because of terrorism.

How Can You Help?

You can donate money or supplies to a local SAR organization. Many search and rescue teams are made up of volunteers. They receive no pay for their work. The human handlers usually pay for all the animals' expenses too, like food, vet bills, training, and certification.

You can learn more about SAR organizations at these sites:

https://www.akc.org/dogny/grants.cfm
http://www.sardogsus.org/id15.html

When there is a natural disaster or other large scale event that requires SAR teams, you can volunteer to provide food and other supplies that the teams need to stay focused on the job.

You can write an essay or do a school project to make others aware of how important SAR animals are in emergency situations.

Glossary

assist (uh-SISST): to help someone

avalanche (AV-uh-lanch): a large snow and ice pack that slides quickly down a mountain

canines (KAY-ninez): another word for dogs

drowning (DROUN-ing): when under water, dying from lack of air

equine (ek- WINE): another word for horse or having to do with horses

first responders (FURST ri-SPOND-urz): rescue, firefighters, or police officers who are the first to arrive at the scene of an accident

impulses (IM-puhlss-ez): pulses or jolts of energy

laboratory (LAB-ruh-tor-ee): a room or building that has scientific equipment so people can do science experiments or tests

scent (SENT): odor or trail of a person or animal

skin cells (SKIN SELZ): microscopic parts of skin

training (TRANE-ing): teaching an animal or person how to do something

volunteers (vol-uhn-TIHRZ): people who do a job without getting paid for the job

Index

Show What You Know

1. How long does it usually take to train a SAR dog?
2. Where can SAR dogs work?
3. How do SAR dogs help rescue workers?
4. Why are SAR dogs so valuable on rescue missions?
5. How do SAR teams use horses on missions?

Websites to Visit

jcsda.com/kids

www.timeforkids.com/photos-video/video/dogs-rescue-25761

www.scholastic.com/browse/article.jsp?id=5242

About the Author

Precious McKenzie is a writer and animal lover who lives in Montana. She shares her home (and yard) with two dogs, two cats, six chickens, and a horse.

Meet The Author!
www.meetREMauthors.com

www.rourkeeducationalmedia.com

PHOTO CREDITS: Cover: ©deepspacedave; cover (top): ©unasmith; cover (bottom): ©Maslov Dmitry; title page: ©FEMA/Michael Riger; page 4: ©F.undT.Werner; page 5 (top): ©TACrafts; page 5 (middle), page 6 (bottom), page 20: ©FEMA/Jocelyn Augustino; page 5 (bottom): ©Digital Storm; page 6 (top), page 14 ©FEMA; page 7 (top): ©bluecrayola; page 7 (middle): ©Cyncoclub; page 7 (bottom): ©Beba73; page 8: ©Lenkadon; page8-9: ©Rafat; page 9: ©LukaTDB; page 10 (top): ©Natykach Nataliia; page 10 (bottom): ©FEMA/Marvin Nauman; page 11: ©MarkRose; page 12: ©FEMA/Andrea Booher; page 13: ©photosbyjim; page 15 (top): ©DNY59; page 15 (middle): ©dreamzdesigner; page 15 (middle): ©bikeriderlondon; page 15 (bottom): ©JorgeHackmann; page 17: ©Emert; page 18: ©Wikipedia; page 19: ©photobobs; page 21 (top): ©vividsen; page 21 (middle): ©xalanx ; page 21 (bottom): ©cathy yeulet

Edited by: Luana Mitten

Cover design by: Jen Thomas
Interior design by: Rhea Magaro

Library of Congress PCN Data

Search and Rescue Animals/Precious McKenzie
 (Animal Matters)
  ISBN 978-1-63430-067-4(hard cover)
  ISBN 978-1-63430-097-1 (soft cover)
  ISBN 978-1-63430-123-7 (e-Book)
 Library of Congress Control Number: 2014953371

Printed in the United States of America, North Mankato, Minnesota

Also Available as: